THE TOMTEN

Adapted by Astrid Lindgren
from a poem by Viktor Rydberg
illustrations by Harald Wiberg

With a keen sense of the warmth and charm that children love, Astrid Lindgren tells the story of the Tomten, the little troll who walks around a lonely old farmhouse at night talking to all the animals.

The story of THE TOMTEN is adapted by the author, from a poem written by Viktor Rydberg, a well-known 19th-century Swedish writer.

In Sweden, Astrid Lindgren ranks among the finest contemporary writers of children's books. In 1958 she was awarded the Hans Christian Andersen Medal at the Fifth Conference of the International Board on Books for Young People in Florence. The Nils Holgersson Plaque is the finest mark of distinction in Sweden for any writer of books for children and young people. Its first award went to Astrid Lindgren.

The author brings affection and tenderness to this simple tale. There is silence and beauty here, too, for it seems as if the Tomten is the only one awake on this cold, snowy night. While the farm sleeps he walks about with a friendly word for each farm animal.

Appealing, delicate, lovely—all these apply to the illustrations of Harald Wiberg for this book. Against a background of frosty winter scenes, the artist contrasts the warmth and friendliness of the Tomten as he visits each animal, speaking in tomten language which only the animals can understand. The foremost painter of animals and nature in Sweden, Mr Wiberg originally made these illustrations for his sons, taken from the lonely farm where the artist was born. They were first published in a children's magazine with the original poem by Viktor Rydberg. Mr Wiberg graduated from the Academy of Arts in Stockholm.

THE TOMTEN possesses that rare spark that makes a children's book a classic — the perfect blending of an author and artist with the same qualities of warmth, tenderness, exceptional talent and a special feeling for the story.

The Tomten

ADAPTED BY ASTRID LINDGREN FROM A POEM BY VIKTOR RYDBERG

ILLUSTRATED BY HARALD WIBERG

COWARD-McCANN, INC., NEW YORK

Library of Congress Catalog Card Number: 61—10658

Printed in Sweden by Tiden-Barnängen tryckerier ab Stockholm 1964

It is the dead of night. The old farm lies fast asleep and everyone inside the house is sleeping too.

The farm is deep in the middle of the forest. Once upon a time someone came here, cut down trees, built a homestead and farmed the land. No one knows who. The stars are shining in the sky tonight, the snow lies white all around, the frost is cruel. On such a night people creep into their small houses, wrap themselves up and bank the fire on the hearth.

Here is a lonely old farm where everyone is sleeping. All but one…

The Tomten is awake. He lives in a corner of the hayloft and comes out at night when human beings are asleep. He is an old, old tomten who has seen the snow of many hundreds of winters. No one knows when he came to the farm. No one has ever seen him, but they know he is there. Sometimes when they wake up they see the prints of his feet in the snow. But no one has seen the Tomten.

On small silent feet the Tomten moves about in the moonlight. He peeps into cowshed and stable, storehouse and toolshed. He goes between the buildings making tracks in the snow.

The Tomten goes first to the cowshed. The cows are dreaming that summer is here, and they are grazing in the fields. The Tomten talks to them in tomten language, a silent little language the cows can understand.

> *"Winters come and winters go,*
>
> *Summers come and summers go,*
>
> *Soon you can graze in the fields."*

The moon is shining into the stable. There stands Dobbin, thinking. Perhaps he remembers a clover field, where he trotted around last summer. The Tomten talks to him in tomten language, a silent little language a horse can understand.

> *"Winters come and winters go,*
>
> *Summers come and summers go,*
>
> *Soon you will be in your clover field."*

Now all the sheep and lambs are sleeping soundly. But they bleat softly when the Tomten peeps in at the door. He talks to them in tomten language, a silent little language the sheep can understand.

"*All my sheep, all my lambs,*

   The night is cold, but your wool is warm,

   And you have aspen leaves to eat."

Then on small silent feet the Tomten goes to the chicken house,

and the chickens cluck contentedly when he comes. He talks to them

in tomten language, a silent little language chickens can understand.

"Lay me an egg, my jolly chickens, and I will give you corn to eat."

The dog kennel roof is white with snow, and inside is Caro. Every night he waits for the moment when the Tomten will come. The Tomten is his friend, and he talks to Caro in tomten language, a silent little language a dog can understand.

"Caro, my friend, is it cold tonight? Are you cold in your kennel? I'll fetch more straw and then you can sleep."

The house where the people live is silent. They are sleeping through

the winter night without knowing that the Tomten is there.

> "*Winters come and winters go,*
>
> *I have seen people large and small*
>
> *But never have they seen me,*" thinks the Tomten.

He tiptoes across to the children's cot, and stands looking for a long time.

"If they would only wake up, then I could talk to them in tomten language, a silent little language children can understand. But children sleep at night."

And away goes the Tomten on his little feet. In the morning the children see his tracks, a line of tiny footprints in the snow.

Then the Tomten goes back to his cozy little corner in the hayloft. There, in the hay, the cat is waiting for him, for she wants milk. The Tomten talks to the cat in tomten language, a silent little language a cat can understand.

"Of course you may stay with me, and of course I will give you milk," says the Tomten.

Winter is long and dark and cold, and sometimes the Tomten

dreams of summer.

"*Winters come and winters go,*

Summers come and summers go,

Soon the swallows will be here," thinks the Tomten.

But the snow still lies in deep drifts around the old farm in the forest. The stars shine in the sky, it is biting cold. On such a night people creep into their small houses and bank the fire on the hearth.

Here is a lonely old farm, where everyone is fast asleep. All but one...

Winters come and summers go, year follows year, but as long as people live at the old farm in the forest, every night the Tomten will trip around between the houses on his small silent feet.